America the Beautiful

Katharine Lee Bates

Samuel A. Ward

1. O beau-ti-ful for spa-cious skies, For am-ber waves of grain,___ For
2. O beau-ti-ful for pil-grim feet Whose stern im-pas-sion'd stress___ A
3. O beau-ti-ful for he-roes prov'd In lib-er-at-ing strife,___ Who
4. O beau-ti-ful for pa-triot dream, That sees be-yond the years___ Thine

pur-ple moun-tain maj-es-ties A-bove the fruit-ed plain.___ A-
thor-ough-fare for free-dom beat A-cross the wil-der-ness.___ A-A-
more than self their coun-try lov'd And mer-cy more than life.___ A-A-
al-a-bas-ter cit-ies gleam, Un-dimmed by hu-man tears.___ A-

mer-i-ca! A-mer-i-ca! God shed His grace on thee,___ And
mer-i-ca! A-mer-i-ca! God mend thine ev-'ry flaw,___ Con-
mer-i-ca! A-mer-i-ca! May God thy gold re-fine___ Till
mer-i-ca! A-mer-i-ca! God shed His grace on thee,___ And

crown thy good with broth-er-hood From sea to shin-ing sea.
firm thy soul in self-con-trol, Thy lib-er-ty in law.
all suc-cess be no-ble-ness, And ev-'ry gain di-vine.
crown thy good with broth-er-hood From sea to shin-ing sea.

MAR 1994

America
the
Beautiful

Atheneum   1993   New York

Maxwell Macmillan Canada
Toronto

AMERICA
the
BEAUTIFUL

Katharine Lee Bates
illustrated by Neil Waldman

Maxwell Macmillan International
New York   Oxford   Singapore   Sydney

Atheneum
Macmillan Publishing Company
866 Third Avenue
New York, NY 10022

Maxwell Macmillan Canada, Inc.
1200 Eglinton Avenue East
Suite 200
Don Mills, Ontario M3C 3N1

Macmillan Publishing Company is part of the
Maxwell Communication Group of Companies.

First edition
Printed in Singapore
10 9 8 7 6 5 4 3 2 1
The text of this book is set in 27 point Windsor Light.
The illustrations are rendered in acrylic paints.

Library of Congress Cataloging-in-Publication Data

Bates, Katharine Lee, 1859–1929.
America the beautiful / by Katharine Lee Bates; illustrated by
Neil Waldman.—1st ed.
p.   cm.
Summary: An illustrated edition of the nineteenth-century poem,
later set to music, celebrating the beauty of America.
ISBN 0-689-31861-8
1. United States—Juvenile poetry.   2. Children's poetry,
American.   [1. United States—Poetry.   2. American poetry.
3. Songs—United States.]   I. Waldman, Neil, ill.   II. Title.
PS1077.B4A8   1993
811'.4—dc20   92-46199

Foreword

The seeds for this book were planted many years ago when I lived on a communal farm in Israel. I had gone to visit my friend Moti Shuval in his room after a long, hot day of avocado picking, and as we sat talking, the subject of travel came up.

"How would you like to see the United States together?" Moti asked me.

"I don't know," I answered. After all, I had left the United States to live in Israel after college and had no plans to return then. But Moti persisted. He filled my head with visions of beautiful places until I finally succumbed. Strange, I thought, to be convinced to see my own country by a foreigner.

In the following weeks and months, we planned our trip. We would drive in a huge rectangle from New York, west through the northern Rockies to the Pacific Northwest, then down the entire Pacific Coast, and back through the Southwest and the South. We flew into New York in late June and set out three weeks later in an old Chevy station wagon.

As we drove west through the flatlands of Indiana and Ohio, I was filled with a sense of anticipation and excitement. In the following weeks, I was never disappointed, for we came upon innumerable places of natural wonder, each more magnificent than the last. When we finally returned to New York that fall, we had driven thirteen thousand miles and witnessed beauty beyond the realm of imagination.

In the years since, I have traveled to four continents and more than a score of countries, but nothing I have seen can match the magnificent splendor that lies within our own borders.

The paintings in this book are a visual record of that first cross-country trip, for all these landscapes reflect places we saw then...all thanks to a little redheaded foreigner named Moti Shuval.

Neil Waldman

O beautiful

for spacious skies,

For amber waves of grain,

For purple mountain majesties

Above the fruited plain!

America!

America!

God shed His grace on thee

And crown thy good

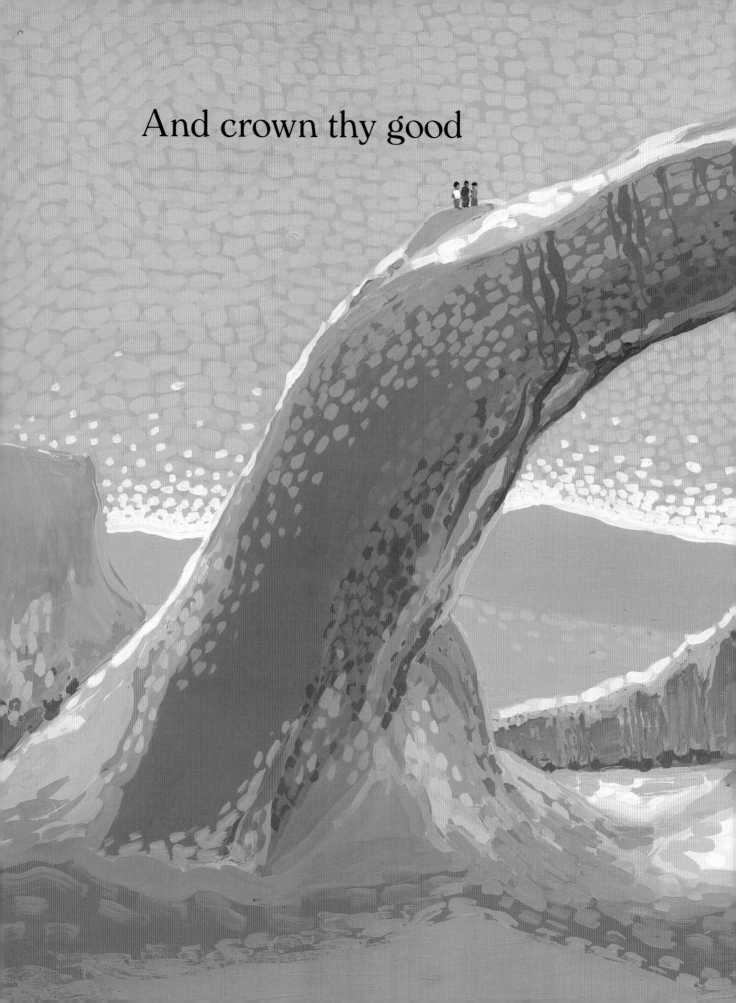

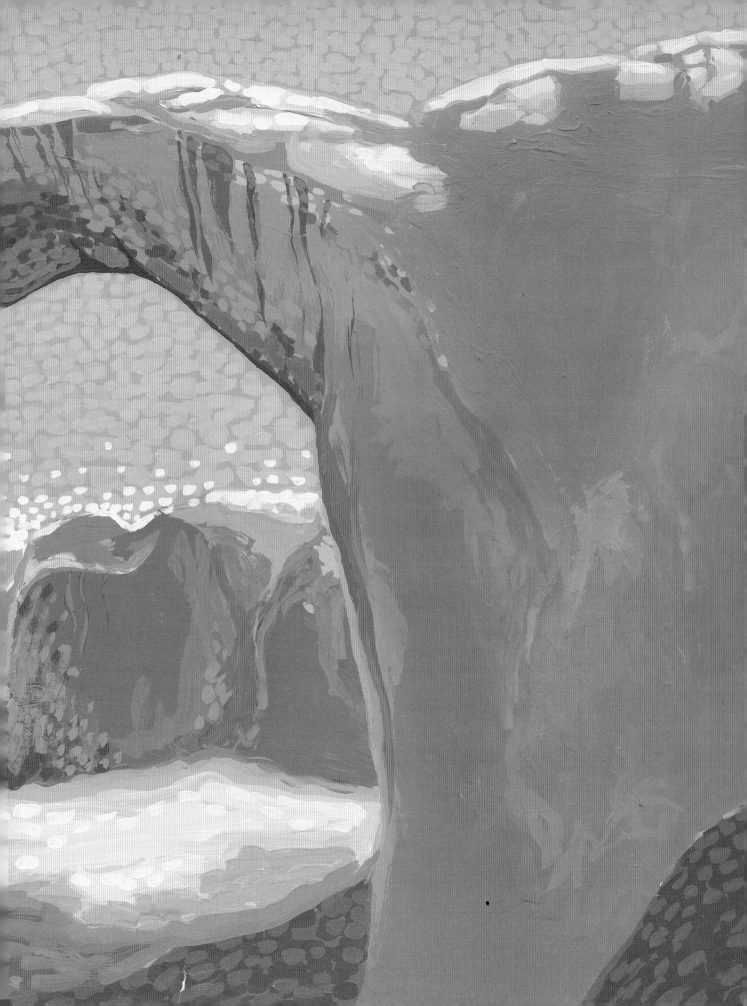

with brotherhood

From sea

to shining sea!

Monument Valley
This flat plain in Utah and Arizona is filled with beautiful sandstone formations that rise like huge sculptures from the valley floor.

Niagara Falls
These "Thundering Waters," as the Native Americans called them, are found on the Canadian border of New York State. Approximately two hundred thousand cubic feet of water pours over the falls each second.

The Great Smoky Mountains
This range of mountains in Tennessee derives its name from the misty haze that always seems to rest between its mountain peaks.

The Great Plains
The American bison, which thundered in great herds across the entire American continent before the first Europeans arrived, were driven to near extinction in the Great Plains by the white man's wanton killing. These buffalo have since been reestablished in many western states; today, several large herds can be seen in Yellowstone and other national parks.

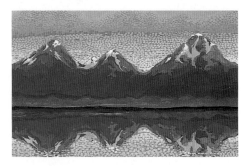

The Grand Tetons
A spectacular chain of mountains in northern Wyoming, their peaks remain snow covered even in summer. Grand Teton, the tallest peak, is nearly fourteen thousand feet high.

Napa Valley

This rich and beautiful valley in central California provides ideal conditions for growing grapes, which are harvested each year by migrant workers. Many of the world's fine wines originate here.

The Grand Canyon

One of the most awe-inspiring sites in the world, this immense gorge has been carved out by the wild and twisting Colorado River, which cuts through its center. At the bottom of the canyon lies the oldest exposed rock on earth.

The Coastal Redwoods

Found in northern California and Oregon, these ancient trees are the tallest living things on earth. They reach heights of more than two hundred feet.

Mesa Verde

Located in the four-corner area, where Colorado, Utah, Arizona, and New Mexico meet, these ancient cliff dwellings were built into the walls of a magnificent canyon by a prehistoric tribe of Native Americans.

Rainbow Bridge

This natural rock sculpture is found just north of the Arizona-Utah border, in the Red Rock Desert. It is the largest natural bridge in the world, spanning the distance of an entire football field. It sits in the land of the Navajo, who called it "Rainbow Across the Sky."

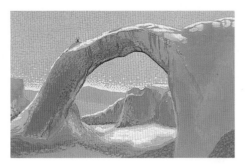

Mount Rushmore

This giant sculpture by Gutzon Borglum is carved into the rock of the Black Hills of South Dakota. Begun in 1927, it took fourteen years to complete and portrays the heads of Washington, Jefferson, Lincoln, and Theodore Roosevelt. The heads are more than sixty feet high.

Oregon Coast

One of the world's most amazing stretches of coastline, it is filled with angular rock formations and wonderful tide pools, where one can examine tiny worlds of ocean life at close range.

Statue of Liberty

Majestically standing on an island in New York Harbor, this great copper statue by Frédéric-Auguste Bartholdi was a gift from the French people, commemorating the centennial of America's independence. For more than a century, it has welcomed immigrants to our shores from around the world.

Pikes Peak

In 1893 the magnificent hundred-mile view from the summit inspired Katharine Lee Bates to write the words to the poem "America the Beautiful."